R0083749713

12/2015

 **W9-BIP-908**

A Beginning-to-Read Book

Dear Dragon Goes to the Police Station

by Margaret Hillert

Illustrated by Jack Pullan

NORWOOD HOUSE PRESS

DEAR CAREGIVER, The *Beginning-to-Read* series is a carefully written collection of classic readers you may remember from your own childhood. Each book features text comprised of common sight words to provide your child ample practice reading the words that appear most frequently in written text. The many additional details in the pictures enhance the story and offer the opportunity for you to help your child expand oral language and develop comprehension.

Begin by reading the story to your child, followed by letting him or her read familiar words and soon your child will be able to read the story independently. At each step of the way, be sure to praise your reader's efforts to build his or her confidence as an independent reader. Discuss the pictures and encourage your child to make connections between the story and his or her own life. At the end of the story, you will find reading activities and a word list that will help your child practice and strengthen beginning reading skills.

Above all, the most important part of the reading experience is to have fun and enjoy it!

Shannon Cannon

Shannon Cannon, Ph.D.
Literacy Consultant

Norwood House Press • P.O. Box 316598 • Chicago, Illinois 60631
For more information about Norwood House Press please visit our website at
www.norwoodhousepress.com or call 866-565-2900.

Text copyright ©2015 by Margaret Hillert. Illustrations and cover design copyright ©2015 by Norwood House Press, Inc. All rights reserved. No part of this book may be reproduced or utilized in any form or by any means without written permission from the publisher.

LIBRARY OF CONGRESS CATALOGING-IN-PUBLICATION DATA
Hillert, Margaret.
  Dear Dragon goes to the police station / by Margaret Hillert ; illustrated by Jack Pullan.
    pages cm. -- (A Beginning-to-read book)
  Summary: "A boy and his pet dragon go on a class trip to the local police station.
They learn about police officers and how they keep us safe. This title includes reading
activities and a word list"-- Provided by publisher.
  ISBN 978-1-59953-676-7 (library edition : alk. paper) -- ISBN
978-1-60357-736-6 (ebook)
  [1. Police stations--Fiction. 2. Dragons--Fiction.] I. Pullan, Jack, illustrator. II. Title.
  PZ7.H558Degj 2015
  [E]--dc23
                                              2014030325

262N—122014
Manufactured in the United States of America in North Mankato, Minnesota.

It's a good day for a walk.
We will go for a walk to the police station.

Police station! Police station!
Why?
Did we do something bad?

No, no, no.
The police are good friends.
They like to see us.
We like to see them.

We have to do this so
we can all cross the street.

The light is red.
We have to stop.

Now it is green
so we can go.

Here is the police station.
We can go in here.

Come in.
Come in.
We are happy to see you.

This is our dog, Sarge.
He helps us find lost kids.

We have a horse, too.
His name is Brownie.
He works outside.
Sometimes you see him in a parade.

We use this car.
It has red and blue lights.
It can go fast.

Sometimes we use this.
It can go pretty fast too.

This is where we work.
People call us for help.

I see what you have.
You help people stay safe.

We help people too.

Now I have something for you.
A book for you to read and color.

And here are some play badges.

It was fun to be here,
but it is time for us to go.

We were happy to see you.
Soon we will come to
see you at your school.

Here you are with me,
and here I am with you.
Oh what a good, good day,
Dear Dragon!

READING REINFORCEMENT

The following activities support the findings of the National Reading Panel that determined the most effective components for reading instruction are: Phonemic Awareness, Phonics, Vocabulary, Fluency, and Text Comprehension.

Phonemic Awareness: The /p/ sound

Substitution: Ask your child to say the following words without the /**p**/ sound:

pat - /p/ = at	peel - /p/ = eel	Pam - /p/ = am
pit - /p/ = it	pin - /p/ = in	pant - /p/ = ant
pair - /p/ = air		

Phonics: The letter Ss

1. Demonstrate how to form the letters **S** and **s** for your child.
2. Have your child practice writing **S** and **s** at least three times each.
3. Ask your child to point to the words in the book that have the letter **s**.
4. Write down the following words and ask your child to circle the letter **s** in each word:

see	saw	basket	sit	bears
pass	is	shapes	star	Sam
kiss	said	say	something	house
was	she	sun		

Vocabulary: Adjectives

1. Explain to your child that words that describe something are called adjectives.

2. Say the following nouns and ask your child to name an adjective that might be used to describe it (possible answers in parentheses):

   car (fast)   marble (round)   dog (soft)

   flower (pretty)   coin (shiny)   crayon (little)

   apple (juicy)   sun (bright)   ice (cold)

3. Write the nouns on separate pieces of paper.

4. Randomly place the pieces of paper on a flat surface. Read each noun aloud to your child. Ask your child to point to the correct word.

5. Encourage your child to think of other adjectives that can describe each noun.

Fluency: Shared Reading

1. Reread the story to your child at least two more times while your child tracks the print by running a finger under the words as they are read. Ask your child to read the words he or she knows with you.

2. Reread the story taking turns, alternating readers between sentences or pages.

Text Comprehension: Discussion Time

1. Ask your child to retell the sequence of events in the story.

2. To check comprehension, ask your child the following questions:

   • When a stoplight is red, what should you do?

   • What type of animal is Sarge? What does he help Police Officers do?

   • What kinds of things can you find at a Police Station?

Dear Dragon Goes to the Police Station uses the **99** words listed below. The **8** words bolded below serve as an introduction to new vocabulary, while the other 91 are pre-primer. You may wish to write the words on index cards and use them to help your child build automatic word recognition. Regular practice with these words will enhance your child's fluency in reading connected text.

a	day	I	read
all	dear	in	red
am	did	is	
and	do	it	**safe**
are	**dog**	it's	Sarge
at	dragon		school
		kids	see
bad	fast		so
badges	find	light(s)	some
be	for	like	something
blue	friends	lost	sometimes
book	fun		soon
Brownie		me	**station**
but	go		stay
	good	name	stop
call	green	no	**street**
can		now	
car	happy		the
color	has	oh	them
come	have	our	they
cross	he	outside	this
	help(s)		time
	here	**parade**	to
	him	people	too
	his	play	
	horse	**police**	
		pretty	

us
use
walk
was
we
were
what
where
why
will
with
work(s)
you
your

ABOUT THE AUTHOR

Margaret Hillert has written over 80 books for children who are just learning to read. Her books have been translated into many different languages and over a million children throughout the world have read her books. She first started writing poetry as a child and has continued to write for children and adults throughout her life. A first grade teacher for 34 years, Margaret is now retired from teaching and lives in Michigan where she likes to write, take walks in the morning, and care for her three cats.

Photograph by Glenna Washburn

ABOUT THE ILLUSTRATOR

A talented and creative illustrator, Jack Pullan, is a graduate of William Jewell College. He has also studied informally at Oxford University and the Kansas City Art Institute. He was mentored by the renowned watercolor artists, Jim Hamil and Bill Amend. Jack's work has graced the pages of many enjoyable children's books, various educational materials, cartoon strips, as well as many greeting cards. Jack currently resides in Kansas.